A Moving World

By Nicolas Brasch

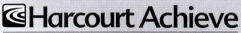
Rigby • Saxon • Steck-Vaughn

www.HarcourtAchieve.com
1.800.531.5015

PM Extensions Nonfiction
Sapphire

U.S. Edition © 2013 Houghton Mifflin Harcourt Publishing Company
125 High Street
Boston, MA 02110
www.hmhco.com

Text © 2004 Cengage Learning Australia Pty Limited
Illustrations © 2004 Cengage Learning Australia Pty Limited
Originally published in Australia by Cengage Learning Australia

All rights reserved. No part of this work may be reproduced or transmitted in any form or by any means, electronic or mechanical, including photocopying or recording, or by any information storage and retrieval system, without the prior written permission of the copyright owner unless such copying is expressly permitted by federal copyright law. Requests for permission to make copies of any part of the work should be submitted through our Permissions website at https://customercare.hmhco.com/contactus/Permissions.html or mailed to Houghton Mifflin Harcourt Publishing Company, Attn: Rights Compliance and Analysis, 9400 Southpark Center Loop, Orlando, Florida 32819-8647.

6 7 8   1957   20
29113

Text: Nicolas Brasch
Printed in China by 1010 Printing International Ltd

A Moving World
ISBN 978 0 75 789260 8

Contents

Introduction		4
Chapter 1	The Center of Earth	6
Chapter 2	The Moving Continents	10
Chapter 3	Ice, Ice, Ice	16
Chapter 4	Waves and Tides	22
Chapter 5	Cliffs and Sand Dunes	26
Chapter 6	Moving Through Space	28
Chapter 7	The Journey's End	31
Glossary		32
Index		

Introduction

Bubbling, whizzing, and spinning

If you stand still, totally still, and don't move a muscle, you're not really still. You're actually moving around and around, from side to side, and up and down. That's because Earth is constantly moving.

Far beneath your feet, the earth is bubbling, spinning, and crashing together. All around you, it is swirling and colliding. It is even whizzing through space. When it comes to Earth, there is no such thing as complete stillness.

It's enough to make you dizzy!

A journey

This book is going to take you on a journey. The journey begins far beneath us, at the center of Earth. Humans have never set foot here. We are going to travel through the different parts of Earth toward the surface, looking at the different types of movement that occur. Once on the surface, we will look at the world around us. From there we will travel into space and see how Earth moves through space.

So buckle up tight! It's going to be an amazing journey!

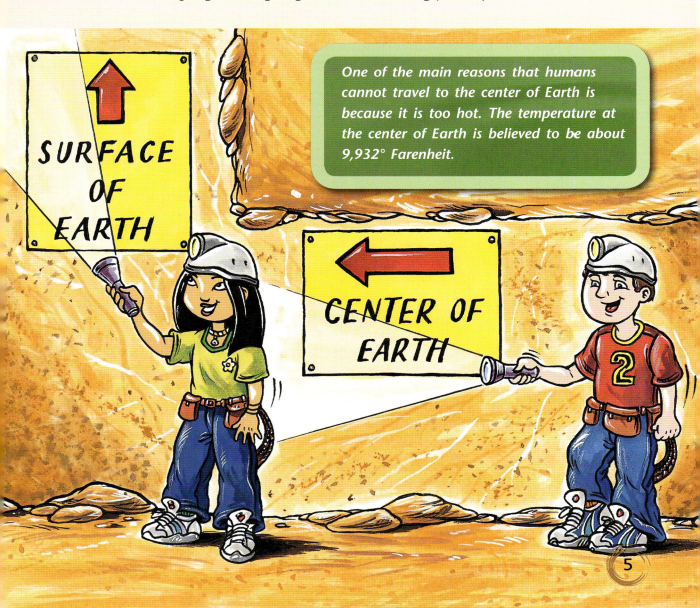

One of the main reasons that humans cannot travel to the center of Earth is because it is too hot. The temperature at the center of Earth is believed to be about 9,932° Farenheit.

CHAPTER 1

The Center of Earth

Constant movement

No one has ever traveled to the center of Earth. Thanks to the work of scientists, we know what we would most likely find there. We would be tossed and twirled around from the **constant** movement that takes place.

There are four main sections that make up Earth beneath the surface:

- inner core
- outer core
- mantle
- crust

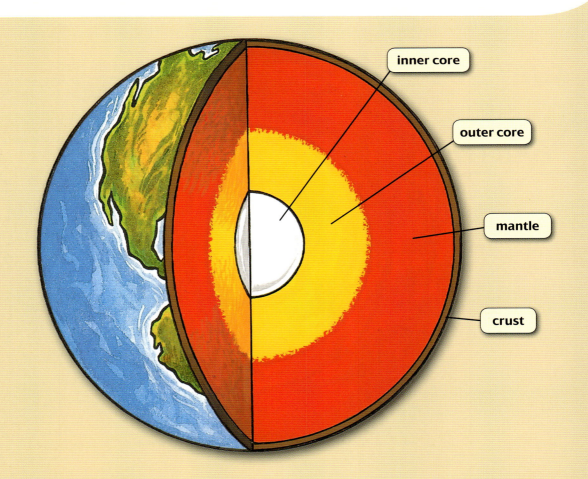

The inner core

The very center of Earth is called the inner core. The inner core is a solid ball of **iron** and **nickel**. It is about 1,430 miles in **diameter**, which is about three-quarters the size of the moon. Surrounding the inner core is the outer core. The outer core is also made up of iron and nickel. However the outer core is a liquid, not a solid. Being surrounded by liquid allows the inner core to spin around and around. The inner core spins in the same direction as Earth is spinning, but a little bit faster.

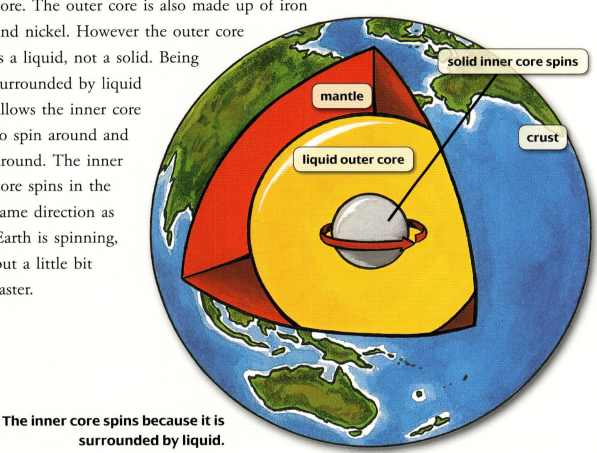

The inner core spins because it is surrounded by liquid.

Journey to the Center of Earth

In 1864 a French writer named Jules Verne wrote a **science-fiction** book called **Journey to the Center of the Earth.** The book describes a journey through a hole and down to Earth's center.

The outer core

The outer core is about 1,430 miles thick. The movement of the iron in the outer core creates electricity. This causes **currents** to travel through Earth. These currents form Earth's magnetic field. The magnetic field is an area around Earth that attracts materials toward it.

The mantle

The mantle surrounds the outer core. The mantle is about 1,800 miles thick and is made up of iron, magnesium, aluminum, silicon, and oxygen. The mantle is solid in most places, but is sticky or like plastic in places where it is very hot. There is constant heat running through the mantle from the inner and outer cores. This heat causes movement known as **convection** currents.

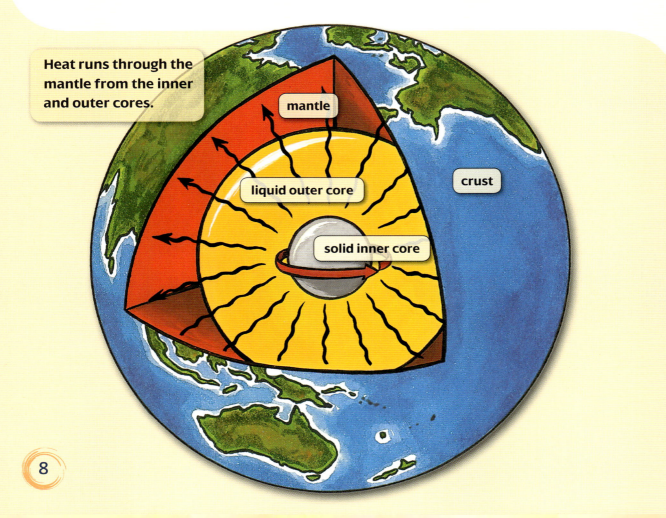

Heat runs through the mantle from the inner and outer cores.

The crust

The area of Earth surrounding the mantle is known as the crust. The crust is made from solid rock and it lies immediately underneath the oceans and continents. It is about 22 miles thick underneath the continents and 3 miles thick underneath the oceans. The crust is very **fragile**. **Faults** in the crust can lead to natural events such as volcanic eruptions. Volcanic eruptions occur when **molten lava** formed in Earth's mantle bursts through a fault in the crust.

Measuring volcanoes

If you want to know more about volcanoes, perhaps you should consider becoming a vulcanologist. A vulcanologist is someone whose job it is to study volcanoes.

An eruption of Mount Etna volcano in Italy

CHAPTER 2
The Moving Continents

Sitting on plates

So far we have studied the movement that takes place all the way from the center of Earth to the crust. Before we reach Earth's surface, we are going to have a look at the tectonic plates, which lie just beneath the surface. The continents and oceans sit on these plates. The movement of these plates has caused enormous changes to the map of the world.

A jigsaw puzzle

There was a time when all of the continents on Earth were joined together. There's no one around who remembers those days. In fact there were no humans around then. It was more than 200 million years ago.

If you look at a map of the world, you will see that some of the coastlines of the continents seem to fit together like a jigsaw puzzle. This is a clue that the continents were once joined together. Another clue is the large numbers of plants, minerals, and animals that are very similar to each other, even though they are on different continents.

Land bridges

For some time, scientists believed that land bridges had once joined the continents. They thought this explained how similar animals could be found on different continents. These bridges then collapsed or were washed away. This **theory** was later proved to be wrong.

The African ostrich (above left) looks similar to the South American rhea (above right), which is another clue that the two continents were once joined.

If Africa and South America could be moved, parts of their coastlines would fit together like puzzle pieces

Alfred Wegener

The first scientist to come up with the theory that one giant continent had split into smaller continents was a German **geologist** named Alfred Wegener. Wegener called the giant continent *Pangaea*, which means "all earth."

Wegener lived from 1880 to 1930. However it was not until the 1960s that his theory became accepted. The reason for this was that Wegener had not given a realistic explanation as to how land areas as large as the continents could have moved around the world.

Alfred Wegener

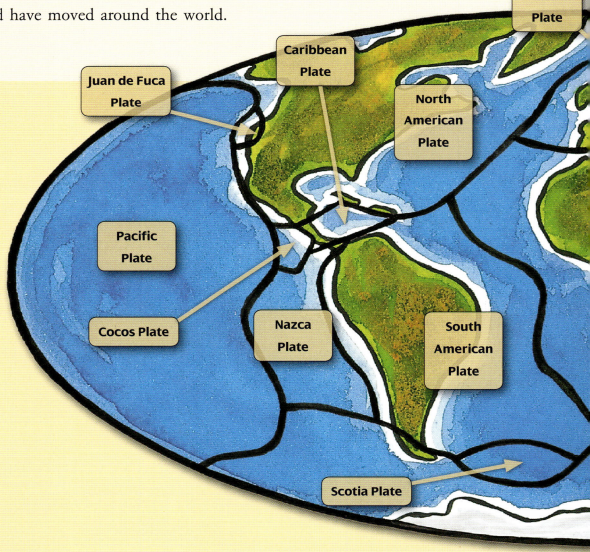

Tectonic plates

By the 1960s, scientists had proved that continents are not fixed in one place but are floating around on plate-like slabs of rock. Even the ocean floors sit on these plates. The scientists named the plates *tectonic plates*. Those carrying land are called *continental plates*, and those carrying the oceans are called *oceanic plates*.

The tectonic plates are not racing around Earth at an incredible speed. They move just a few inches each year.

> There are seven main tectonic plates. These are the African Plate, Antarctic Plate, Eurasian Plate, Indo-Australian Plate, North American Plate, Pacific Plate, and South American Plate. There are more than 20 smaller plates.

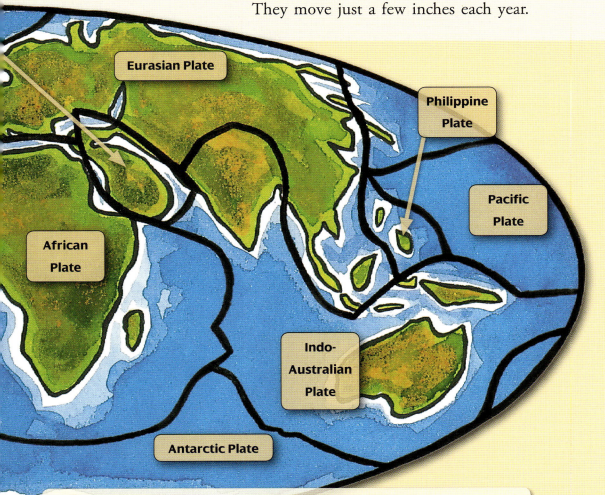

This map shows the main tectonic plates as well as some of the smaller ones.

Colliding, sliding, and passing

When two oceanic plates collide, one of them slides underneath the other one. If an oceanic plate collides with a continental plate, the oceanic plate will slide underneath the continental plate. This forms a deep ocean trench. When two continental plates collide, they form major mountain ranges. They may also form a single continent.

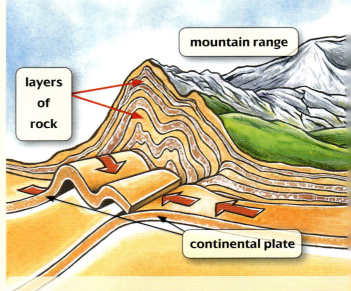

When two continental plates collide, layers of rock are folded up to form a mountain range.

When two plates drift apart, new ocean floor is created. When two plates pass by each other, touching but not colliding, the force causes **earthquakes**. Areas that are regularly hit by earthquakes sit near the edge of a plate, where such movement is common.

Towns and cities can be severely damaged by earthquakes.

A changing map

The constant movement of the plates means that the map of the world is continually changing. In our lifetime the change is so small that it is not noticeable. However, in several million years, the world will look nothing like it does now. Some scientists believe that the continents are gradually moving toward each other and will form another single, giant continent. This continent will be different in shape and location to Pangaea. Just as Pangaea split, the **theory** is that a new giant continent will also split one day, forming brand new continents unlike those that exist today.

> When Pangaea split, it broke into two huge continents, known as **Gondwanaland** and **Laurasia**. Gondwanaland then split to form Australia, India, Antarctica, and parts of Africa, and South America. Laurasia split to form the northern continents on Earth: Europe, North America, and most of Asia.

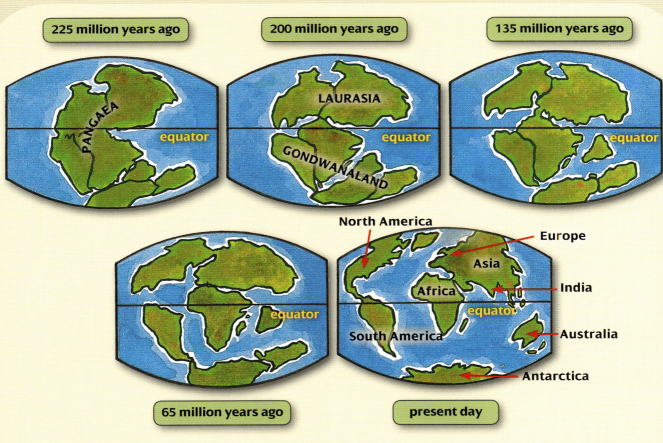

These maps show how the continents formed over hundreds of millions of years.

CHAPTER 3

Ice, Ice, Ice

Covered in ice

We've broken through the surface of Earth in our journey, but it's a bit uncomfortable. We're covered in ice!

Ice currently covers about 3 percent of Earth's total surface and about 10 percent of Earth's land area. However the amount of ice on Earth is constantly changing. The change is not enough for us to notice on a daily basis, but if we were to travel back in time 15,000 years, we would see that about 30 percent of Earth's land was covered by ice. Canada was almost entirely covered by ice, as was northern United States and northern Europe.

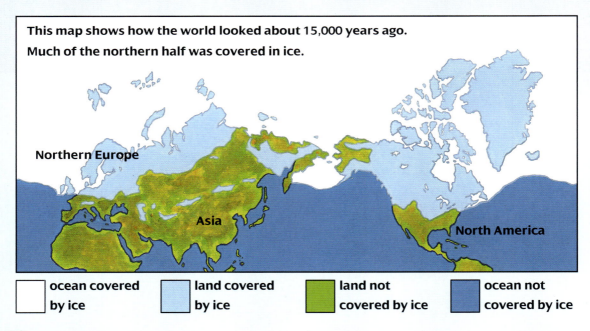

This map shows how the world looked about 15,000 years ago. Much of the northern half was covered in ice.

Glaciers

Glaciers are the most common form of ice that covers Earth. Glaciers are large masses of ice that form when the amount of snow that falls in a particular area is greater than the amount of snow and ice that eventually melts. As a result, a large amount of ice forms. Glaciers always form on land but some of them slide, fall, or break off into the ocean.

Try this!

If you find yourself in an area with snow, you can do an **experiment** that copies how glaciers are formed. Collect a container full of snow. Let some of it melt, just as it would in the open. Then place the rest in a freezer. This will form a mini-glacier.

The Barne Glacier in Antarctica is slowly moving out to sea. It is about 98 feet tall.

Ice sheets, ice caps, and ice shelves

The most common types of glaciers are ice sheets, ice caps, and ice shelves. *Ice sheets* are massive areas of ice that cover land. To be considered an ice sheet, an ice mass must be at least 31,000 square miles in size.

An *ice cap* is similar to an ice sheet but is smaller than 31,000 square miles. The ice that covers the country of Greenland is an ice cap.

An *ice shelf* is a large piece of ice that is attached to land on one side, but extends into the ocean on the other side.

The country of Greenland is covered in ice.

Bigger and bigger

The largest glacier in the world is the ice sheet covering Antarctica. This ice sheet contains about 70 percent of the world's fresh water. Every year the Antarctic ice sheet gets bigger and bigger. This puts pressure on the ice that is at the bottom of the sheet. This ice is squeezed into the Antarctic Ocean.

Ice on the move

There is one feature that all glaciers have in common: they move. Even huge ice sheets move. Glaciers move in one of two ways—they either flow or slide.

Glaciers flow when the weight of ice on one part of the glacier forces the rest of the glacier to move. It is possible for a glacier to flow uphill.

Glaciers slide, when the ice at the bottom of the glacier starts to melt into a slippery liquid. This causes the rest of the glacier to slide along.

Hubbard Glacier in Alaska, where it enters the sea

Changing the environment

A large glacier can dramatically change the environment. A glacier flowing or sliding down a mountainside takes with it enormous amounts of **debris**, including huge boulders and large areas of loose dirt. The shape of a mountain can be quite different once a glacier has moved through it.

Breaking away

Large chunks of ice are constantly breaking off Antarctica. In 2000, a piece of ice broke off the Ross Ice Shelf. This piece was nearly 186 miles long. The constant movement of ice means that the shape and size of Antarctica is always changing.

Part of the ice that broke off the Ross Ice Shelf in 2000

Icebergs

While the various types of glaciers move quite slowly, sometimes just a few inches a day, icebergs move much faster. Icebergs are pieces of ice that have broken off a glacier and fallen into the water. They are carried along by the ocean currents and winds. If you lie on your back in the ocean and allow the currents to move you, you will be moving like an iceberg.

An iceberg near the Antarctic Peninsula

CHAPTER 4

Waves and Tides

Movement of waves

From the cold of the ice, we move to the waves of the oceans. There are two main types of movement that occur in the oceans. One determines the height and **ferocity** of waves. The other creates changes in the water level, known as the tide. Each is caused by different forces.

The movement of waves is easy to explain: it is caused by wind. As the wind blows across the water, waves continue to rise in height until the top of the wave gets ahead of the body of the wave. At that point, the wave crashes.

The highest wave

Waves during storms can reach tremendous heights. The highest wave ever recorded—in 1933—was 118 feet.

top of wave

body of wave

a crashing wave

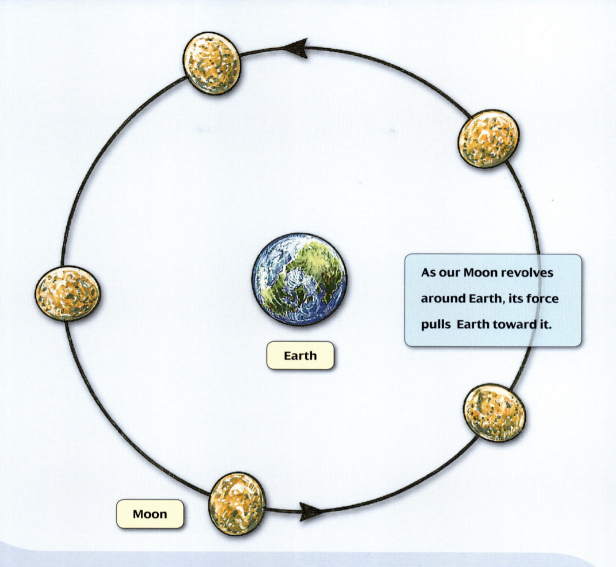

Gravity

The movement of the tides involves gravity. Gravity is the force that pulls objects in a particular direction. For example as Earth moves, it pulls all objects on Earth toward the center of the planet. Without gravity we would be floating all over the place. As the moon **revolves** around Earth, its force pulls Earth toward it. As Earth revolves around the sun, the sun pulls Earth toward it. However Earth's gravity is strong enough to withstand most of the force that comes from the moon and the sun.

High tide

While Earth's force is strong enough to stop objects from floating into space, some movement does occur. An example is the rise and fall of the tides.

The moon's gravity has the greatest effect on Earth's oceans because the moon is much closer to Earth than the sun. As the moon revolves around Earth, the gravity from the moon pulls Earth toward it. This pulling causes a slight bulge along the edge of Earth that is nearest to the moon. The result is a rise in the ocean's water level. This is known as a high tide.

Two high tides a day

On the side of Earth furthest from the moon, there is also a high tide. As Earth is being pulled toward the moon, the ocean that is furthest from the moon is able to stretch out.

Because the moon revolves around Earth once a day, every coastal area on Earth gets two high tides a day. One occurs when the area is closest to the moon and one when it is furthest from the moon.

The highest tides

The highest tides occur during the full moon and new moon. During these moon phases, the moon and the sun form a straight line with Earth. This means that the force of gravity Earth has to deal with is greater than at other times.

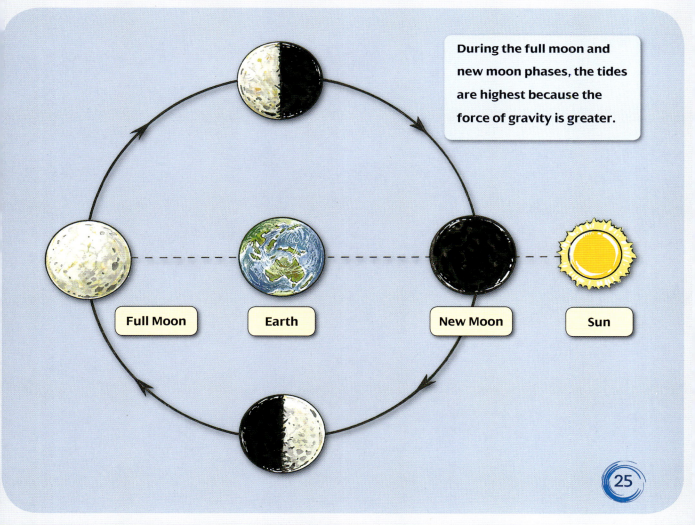

During the full moon and new moon phases, the tides are highest because the force of gravity is greater.

CHAPTER 5

Cliffs and Sand Dunes

Cliffs

Finally we've made it onto dry land. Let's climb up this cliff and think about how it was formed.

Cliffs are formed by the constant crashing of waves against the coastline. This can take thousands of years. Once they are formed, cliffs are constantly changing. Every time a wave crashes against a cliff, it washes away particles of rock. Strong winds blow away materials and eventually cause caves and other holes to appear.

Sand dunes

Sand dunes are formed by wind blowing sand to a particular area. As the amount of sand increases, the sand dune is formed. When these dunes are close to the coast, they can help prevent flooding by stopping water from going too far inland. Some sand dunes are hundreds of feet high and several miles long.

In desert areas, the dunes can move. As dunes become top-heavy, the front of the dune collapses forward. It then builds up in the new spot and collapses forward again. This process takes a long time. You are not likely to see a sand dune chasing someone across the desert!

Forming new landscapes

The materials that are washed or blown away by waves or winds do not disappear. They are swept or blown to new areas where they form new land. This is how beaches, sandbars, ridges, and other types of land are formed.

CHAPTER 6

Moving Through Space

Revolving and spinning

We've seen how things move on and even inside Earth. How about Earth itself? Every second of every day Earth is moving through space. If it stopped moving, we would all fall off the planet. There are two main ways in which Earth moves—it revolves and it spins.

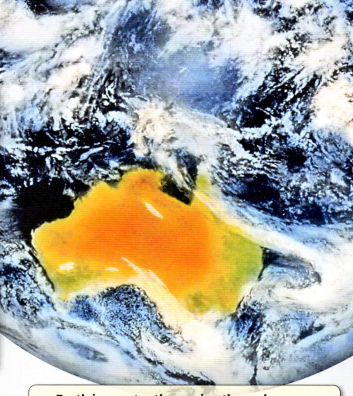

Stop the world, I want to get off!

Earth is constantly moving through space.

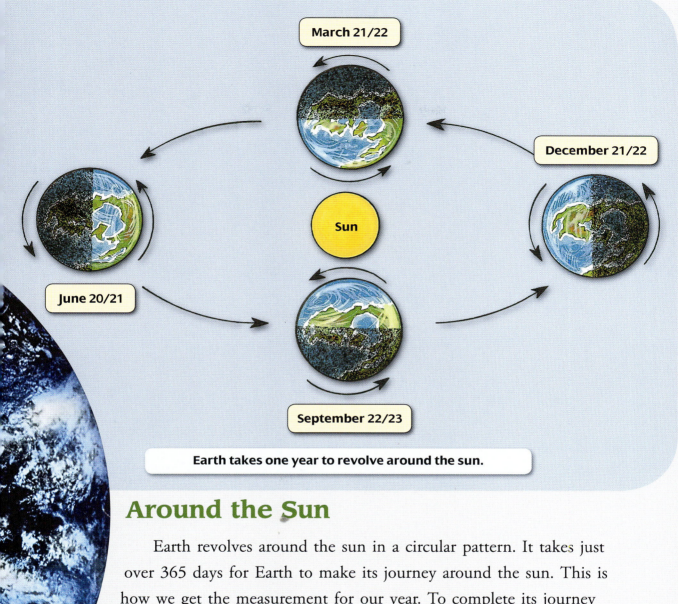

Earth takes one year to revolve around the sun.

Around the Sun

Earth revolves around the sun in a circular pattern. It takes just over 365 days for Earth to make its journey around the sun. This is how we get the measurement for our year. To complete its journey in 365 days, Earth travels at a speed of 67,027 miles an hour.

Faster than a racing car

A racing car reaches a speed of about 186 miles an hour. This means Earth is revolving around the sun 360 times faster than a racing car can go.

Spinning and spinning

As Earth travels around the sun, it also spins on its **axis**. This means that it turns around. If it did not spin, then only one part of Earth would ever be facing the Sun. The rest of Earth would remain in darkness.

The speed at which Earth spins depends on where you are standing. At the extreme ends of Earth, known as the North Pole and South Pole, Earth is not spinning at all. At the places along the middle of Earth, known as the equator, Earth spins at a speed of 1,037 miles an hour.

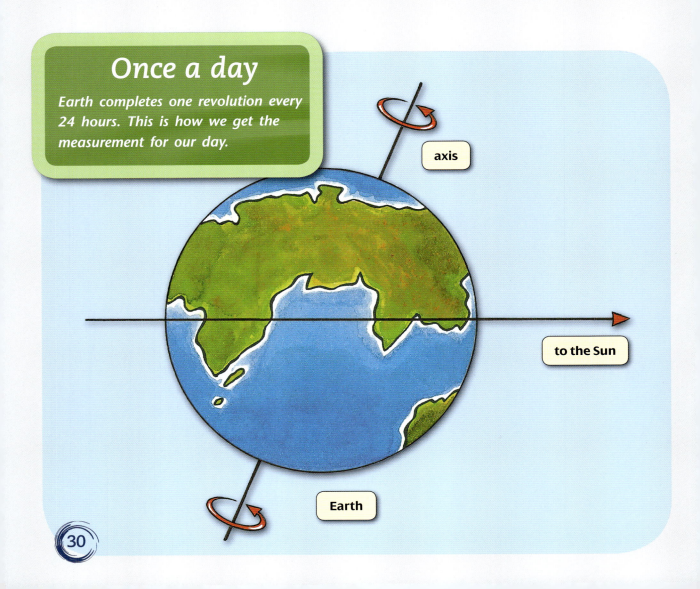

Once a day
Earth completes one revolution every 24 hours. This is how we get the measurement for our day.

CHAPTER 7

The Journey's End

What a fascinating journey! We hope you have enjoyed it. Movement really is fascinating. Who would have thought that every single thing on Earth is constantly moving? It's amazing to think that if Earth suddenly stopped moving, we would all fall off it.

So next time you need to stand perfectly still, do it. But deep down you'll know that you're not really standing still, are you?

Happy spinning!

Glossary

axis	an imaginery line around which an object turns
constant	all the time
convection	the movement of heat in the atmosphere
currents	steady flows of water or air
debris	the remains of something destroyed
diameter	a straight line that passes through the center of a circle or sphere
earthquakes	violent shakings of Earth
experiment	a scientific test
faults	weak spots in Earth's crust
ferocity	great force or power
fragile	easily broken
geologist	someone who studies rock, minerals, and Earth
iron	a heavy metal often used to build structures
molten lava	melted rocks
nickel	a hard, silvery metal
revolves	moves around in a circular motion
science fiction	an imaginery story, often about the future, that involves scientific ideas
theory	a scientific idea used to explore a natural occurrence